MW00964457

a picnic at the Lighthouse

by Rebecca North

illustrated by Nancy Keating

© 2016, Rebecca North

We gratefully acknowledge the financial support of the Canada Council for
the Arts, the Government of Canada through the Canada Book Fund (CBF),
and the Government of Newfoundland and Labrador through the Department of
Business, Tourism, Culture and Rural Development for our publishing program.

All rights reserved. No part of this work covered by the copyrights hereon may
be reproduced or used in any form or by any means—graphic, electronic or
mechanical—without the prior written permission of the publisher. Any requests
for photocopying, recording, taping or information storage and retrieval systems
of any part of this book shall be directed in writing to the Canadian Reprography
Collective, One Yonge Street, Suite 1900, Toronto, Ontario M5E 1E5.

Illustrations by Nancy Keating
Printed on acid-free paper

Published by
TUCKAMORE BOOKS
an imprint of CREATIVE BOOK PUBLISIIING
a Transcontinental Inc. associated company
P.O. Box 8660, Stn. A
St. John's, Newfoundland and Labrador A1B 3T7

Printed in Canada by:
TRANSCONTINENTAL INC.

Library and Archives Canada Cataloguing in Publication

North, Rebecca, 1986-, author
    A picnic at the lighthouse / Rebecca North ; illustrated
by Nancy Keating.

ISBN 978-1-77103-082-3 (paperback)

    I. Keating, Nancy, illustrator II. Title.

PS8627.O783P53 2016   jC813'.6   C2015-907854-7

For Jasper and Peter

– REBECCA

For Jake and his beautiful new son

– NANCY

One day, Patrick and his dad drove to a small town near the ocean to have a picnic next to a lighthouse.

Patrick and his dad walked up a long gravel road to the top of a hill. As they walked, the gravel crunched under Patrick's shoes. The sun felt warm on his shoulders.

A cool, salty breeze blew through his hair. In the sky, seabirds called out to each other.

At the end of the path, they found the big red lighthouse. They walked up to the lighthouse and stood right at the bottom. Patrick looked up. The lighthouse reached all the way up to the clouds. There was a big glass room at the top.

Patrick's dad pointed to the glass room. "When it gets dark or foggy outside, you can see the light shining up there."

"Whoa!" said Patrick. "Hey Dad! Do you want to know what I love the most about today?"

"What do you love the most about today Patrick?"

"This lighthouse! I love this lighthouse!"

Patrick and his dad walked down a path towards the ocean. They found a spot in the grass that was nice and flat. They spread their blanket out on the ground and sat down for their picnic.

Patrick drank some cold lemonade from a glass jar. It was sour and sweet at the same time. It made Patrick's lips pucker. "MMMmmmmmmm!" said Patrick. "Hey Dad! Do you want to know what I love the most about today?"
"What do you love the most about today Patrick?"

"This lemonade! I love lemonade!"

Patrick and his dad sat and looked out at the ocean. "Look out there Patrick! Whales!"

Patrick could see clouds rising up out of the water and then quickly disappearing. "The whales are coming up to breathe," said Patrick's dad.

"Wow!" said Patrick. "Hey Dad! Do you want to know what I love the most about today?"
"What do you love the most about today Patrick?"

"Seeing the whales! I love whales!"

For lunch, Patrick and his dad ate cheese sandwiches on slices of buttered white bread.

Then they ate chocolate cake with sticky sweet icing for dessert.

"YUM!" said Patrick. "Hey Dad! Do you want to know what I love the most about today?"
"What do you love the most about today Patrick?"

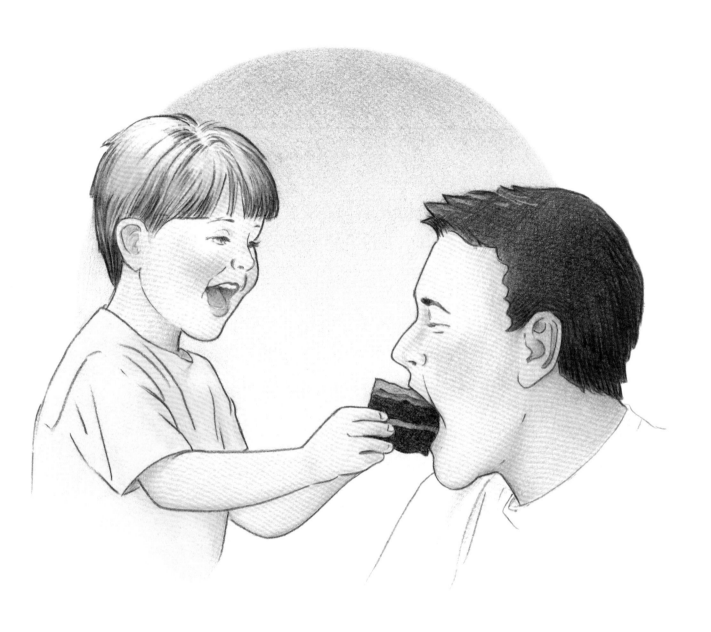

"The chocolate cake! I love chocolate cake!"

After Patrick and his dad finished their lunch, they kept watching the whales in the ocean. Big waves crashed against the rocks.

Patrick started to feel tired. He yawned, lay down on the picnic blanket and looked up at the sky.

Fluffy white clouds floated over their heads. One of them looked like a big whale. Another cloud right next to it looked like a small whale.

Patrick was about to tell his dad about the whale clouds but his eyes got too heavy and he drifted off to sleep.

Patrick's dad scooped him up and carried him back down the gravel road towards the car.

"Hey Patrick, do you want to know what I love the most about today?" asked Patrick's dad. Patrick didn't answer because he was fast asleep.